W9-ARG-664

My Kiss Won't Miss

JAMES RIVER VALLEY
LIBRARY SYSTEM
105 3RD ST SE
JAMESTOWN ND 58401

WITHDRAWN

Lesley Dahlseng
Illustrated by **Mirela Tufan**

WhetWord Press, LLC

WhetWord Press, LLC
PO Box 492
Alexandria, MN 56308

Text copyright © 2014 Lesley Dahlseng
Illustrations copyright © 2014 WhetWord Press, LLC
All rights reserved, including the right of reproduction
in whole or in part in any form.

Book design by Mirela Tufan.
The title text of this book is set in Century Schoolbook.
Inside text is set in BenguiatItcTEE.
The illustrations were digitally rendered.

Printed in China.

Publisher's Cataloging-in-Publication
(Provided by Quality Books, Inc.)
Dahlseng, Lesley.
    My kiss won't miss / Lesley Dahlseng ; illustrated by
Mirela Tufan. -- First edition.
    pages cm
    SUMMARY: In this rhyming story, a little boy sneaks
out of bed and hides, but there is no hiding place to
which a bedtime kiss cannot be blown.
    Audience: Ages 2-5.
    ISBN 978-0-615-98704-0

    1. Bedtime--Juvenile fiction. 2. God (Christianity)
--Juvenile fiction. [1. Bedtime--Fiction. 2. Love--
Fiction. 3. God (Christianity)--Fiction. 4. Stories in
rhyme.] I. Tufan, Mirela, illustrator. II. Title.

PZ8.3.D1363My 2014   [E]
                QBI14-600053

For my daughters, Christina and Katelyn.
And for all children, that they may know the love of God
Who reconciles us unto Himself
L.D.

Night draws near.

The sun can't stay.

Rest now, my Love. Don't run away!

If you should find a place to hide,
Then I will seek you far and wide.

I'll search for you both high and low.
Where did my Beloved go?

Before the sun takes its last bow,
I'll send a bedtime kiss somehow.

Yes... if I can't catch you for a kiss,
I'll *blow* a kiss, and it won't miss!

In beds of flowers by blue streams

My kiss will find you in your dreams.

In blankets made of snowflake lace
My kiss will come and warm your face.

If I can't catch you for a kiss,
I'll *blow* a kiss and it won't miss!

The clouds may hide you in the sky
But you should know, my kisses *fly*!

And if you curl up on the moon,
The stars will guide my kiss there soon.

If I can't catch you for a kiss,
I'll *blow* a kiss and it won't miss!

If nestled in a cozy cave,

Or lulled to sleep on gentle wave,

If on the ocean bed you sleep

My kiss will find you in the deep.

Beyond the golden dunes of sand

My kiss will search throughout the land.

My kiss will scale up mountaintops.
It rides a wind that *never* stops.

It doesn't matter where you are
I'll blow my kiss there from afar.

So snuggle softly in your bed.
Close your eyes and rest your head.

Tuck-tuck now. Out goes the light.
Now in your dreams throughout the night...

The Lord will send His goodnight kiss.

He'll *blow* a kiss and it won't miss!

Nothing
in all creation,
will be able to separate us
from the love of God
that is in Christ Jesus.

(Romans 8:38-39)